D1586521

WORLD WAR I TALES
THE PIGEON SPY

Bloomsbury Education
An imprint of Bloomsbury Publishing Plc

50 Bedford Square
London
WC1B 3DP
UK

1385 Broadway
New York
NY 10018
USA

www.bloomsbury.com

BLOOMSBURY and the Diana logo are trademarks of Bloomsbury Publishing Plc

First published in 2013
This edition published in 2016

Text Copyright © Terry Deary 2013, 2016
Illustrations copyright © James de la Rue 2013
Cover illustration copyright © Chris Mould 2013

Terry Deary and James de la Rue have asserted their rights under the Copyright,
Designs and Patents Act, 1988, to be identified as Author and Illustrator of this work.

This is a work of fiction. Names and characters are the product of the author's imagination
and any resemblance to actual persons, living or dead, is entirely coincidental.

All rights reserved. No part of this publication may be reproduced or transmitted in
any form or by any means, electronic or mechanical, including photocopying, recording,
or any information storage or retrieval system, without prior permission
in writing from the publishers.

No responsibility for loss caused to any individual or organisation acting
on or refraining from action as a result of the material in this publication can
be accepted by Bloomsbury or the author.

A catalogue record for this book is available from the British Library.

ISBN
PB: 978-1-4729-4198-5
ePub: 978-1-4081-9172-9
ePDF: 978-1-4081-9173-6

2 4 6 8 10 9 7 5 3 1

Printed and bound by CPI Group (UK) Ltd, Croydon CR0 4YY

MIX
Paper from
responsible sources
FSC
www.fsc.org   FSC® C020471

This book is produced using paper that is made from wood grown in managed,
sustainable forests. It is natural, renewable and recyclable. The logging and manufacturing
processes conform to the environmental regulations of the country of origin.

To find out more about our authors and books visit www.bloomsbury.com.
Here you will find extracts, author interviews, details of forthcoming events and
the option to sign up for our newsletters.

WORLD WAR I TALES

TERRY DEARY

THE PIGEON SPY

Illustrated by James de la Rue

BLOOMSBURY EDUCATION
AN IMPRINT OF BLOOMSBURY

LONDON OXFORD NEW YORK NEW DELHI SYDNEY

Chapter 1
Doves and dollars

I never left the state of Kansas until I joined the army. In fact, I'd hardly ever left our farm.

'That Great War is nothing to do with us,' Ma used to say. 'You stay out of it, Joe.'

Our farm was a patch of dirt. Dad did the ploughing and sowing – I never liked horses, and they didn't like me. Ma kept the old tractor running and the pick-up truck that got us to Great Bend – every time I touched a machine, it broke. I minded the pigs and chickens, and the pigeons. Maybe you wouldn't think of farming pigeons.

But Ma sold them to Mr Lamarr at his White Dove restaurant in Great Bend to be made into pigeon pie. We needed the money, but I felt bad about the pigeons.

I liked to train my birds to fly back home. Some days I'd run ten miles across the range, then tie a message to the bird's leg and set it free. Those little messages got back to our farm long before I did.

From time to time Ma came back from Great Bend with a newspaper. After dark we'd sit round the oil lamp and read about the Great War over in Europe.

'Looks like America's going to send men across to fight,' Pa said one night in the lamplight.

'Well, they ain't taking my little Joe,' Ma said.

'He has to be eighteen to fight. Joe's only sixteen.'

'He looks eighteen,' Ma argued. 'If the army send men out to look for soldiers you hide in the barn, you hear, Joe?'

Then one day in the spring of 1917 Ma came home wild as a mountain lion. 'Some low-down crook of a farmer over in Dry Walnut Creek is selling Mr Lamarr pigeons for half what we charge. I had to take even less. We'll hardly afford to eat this month,' she sobbed, and tears ran down her thin, sun-stained cheeks. 'All because of this farmer Muller.'

'Muller?' Pa said. 'Sounds German to me.'

'Exactly!' Ma shouted. 'And we're at war with the Germans!'

I tried to remind her: 'You said the Great War is nothing to do with us.'

She wasn't listening. 'It'd serve them right if I sent our Joe to fight them. They'd be beaten inside a week.'

I tried again. 'You said I was too young.'

'I'll drive you in to Great Bend tomorrow. You can sign up for the US Army there.'

'But you said...'

Ma wasn't listening.

We drove into the town the next day and saw a line of men outside the door of the Town Hall. Ma pushed me out of the pick-up truck. I joined the line and shuffled along with the rest till I got to the desk.

'Name?' the man in a khaki uniform asked.

'Joe. Joe Clay.'

'Age?'

'Sixteen.'

The man rubbed his tired eyes. 'We don't take men as young as sixteen. You reckon you mean eighteen?'

'I suppose,' I said. It was a lie. We both knew it.

'I'll put down eighteen,' he said. 'Now put your mark here.'

'I can write my name,' I said proudly.

'That'll come in useful when you're digging trenches,' he muttered. 'Here is a rail pass. Report to Kansas City troop depot a week today and they'll train you up.' He reached out to shake my hand quickly. 'Welcome to the army, son,' he said, then shouted, 'Next!'

And that was how I came to fight in the Great War. All because Ma got in a temper over a few pigeons.

I can't complain. Pigeons got me into the war, but it was a pigeon that got me out of it alive.

Chapter 2
Trains and targets

I went off to Camp Lewis in Washington for training.

First we learned to march. The sergeant said I was the worst marcher he'd ever seen.

Then we tried shooting. My shooting was worse than my marching. When they gave me a rifle everybody hid.

They tried me in the cook house but my porridge was so lumpy the sergeant said it could kill more men than a German machine gun, and my bacon was harder than a bullet.

By the spring of 1918 the army reckoned we were ready to go across the seas to fight the German army. The colonel sent for me. 'Trooper Clay,' he said with a sad shake of his white-haired head. 'What am I going to do with you?'

'Send me to France to fight, sir?'

'You can't shoot straight, you can't march straight, and you can't look after the horses or the trucks.'

'No, sir.'

'We could sent you over to France and tie you to a post. The riflemen could use you for target practice.'

'Yes, sir,' I muttered. My boots were too big and the wool uniform itched and made me sweat. I felt as miserable as a whipped puppy.

'Tell me, Trooper Clay, is there anything you are good at? Any single thing?'

'I can run ten miles in an hour,' I said.

The colonel looked happier. 'That's good. The men in battle need to send messages quickly. Telephone wires get cut or snapped so then they use runners.'

'I could do that,' I said.

'It's a dangerous job,' he said.

My mouth went dry. 'Dangerous?'

'The men in the battle may want supplies. Or they may want to tell our heavy gunners where the enemy troops are, so they can drop shells on them. Now, Trooper Clay, what do the Germans think of that?'

'They don't want the big guns dropping shells on them, sir?'

'Exactly,' the colonel said. 'So your enemy will do all they can to stop the messengers getting through. They send snipers to pick them off. Know what a sniper is?'

'A lone sharp-shooter with a rifle,' I said.

'You'll be trying to run five miles with a message and the sniper will be trying to shoot you. Or they may call up the German Air Force to attack you with planes carrying machine guns. A dangerous job.' The colonel rubbed his hands together. 'Trooper Clay, I'll have you posted to a troop of messengers in France.'

'Thank you sir,' I said. But I don't know why I said that.

Chapter 3

Hawks and hunger

It took eight days to cross the Atlantic Ocean. We landed in a place so green and peaceful I couldn't believe there was a war going on. I was used to the endless flat and dusty plains of Kansas. This was a land of fresh rain, rolling green hills and little fields with sheep and cows.

I said, 'France sure is a great place.'

The sergeant sneered at me. 'We're in England, you dummy.'

The men heard him and laughed. After that no one called me Joe any more – they all called me Dummy.

We spent a couple of weeks in England doing more training. No one was faster than me down the lanes and over the green fields. 'It'll be harder when you get to France,' the sergeant warned me. 'Running in trenches and ditches to stay out of sight, running in darkness or wearing a gas mask.'

I got stronger and my feet got used to the heavy boots. At dinner the other men moaned about how much they hated the army food. I ate everything they put in front of me.

After dinner, some of the men went into the towns on the lorries to drink English beer. But I went down to the other part of the messenger troop: the pigeons.

The soldier in charge of the pigeons was Corporal Bobby Mason – a man nearly as old as Pa, with hair going grey at the sides. He didn't call me Dummy and he listened when I told him about how I trained my birds back home. Now he taught me the way the army did it.

'We get our birds from the pigeon men of Britain,' Corporal Mason told me. 'They're tough little fellers and don't seem to mind the gunfire. Some fly all the way from

France to England. They reckon nineteen out of twenty get through safely.'

'What happens to the others?' I asked.

'The Germans shoot them down, or send up hawks to hunt them. And of course some get eaten by our soldiers.'

'What?' I gasped.

'Every troop takes two or three pigeons into battle. If the men get stuck and their food is cut off, they eat the pigeons. Makes sense,' Bobby told me.

I remembered Mr Lamarr and his White Dove restaurant. I wasn't sure I could eat a pigeon myself, not one that I'd looked after. But, like Bobby said, it made sense if you were hungry.

When I'd been in England a week the corporal said, 'The pigeon trainers they sent me aren't much good. They've never cared for birds before.' He looked away from me.

'What's wrong?' I asked.

'I did something I shouldn't,' he said. 'I went to the sergeant and asked if he could give you a transfer to be a pigeon trainer. He said yes. I hope you don't mind.'

'Mind?' I almost screamed. 'Mind? It's the best job in the army!' I could have kissed the guy.

Of course I didn't know how close the pigeons would come to getting me killed.

Chapter 4

France and friends

I sailed across the English Channel to France and into the Great War. It wasn't all about soldiers stuck in the same trench for years. This was Autumn 1918 and the enemy were being pushed all the way back to Germany.

The British, the French and the Americans were marching forward every day. The Germans kept stopping and turning their machine guns on them. But every day the enemy were driven back.

I had to follow them with the pigeons.

The British called nesting boxes 'pigeon lofts'. I trained the birds to fly back to the lofts. The armies were moving forward, and the lofts were moving with them, every day closer to Germany. And still the birds found their way back.

Every day an army messenger would arrive and pick up a basket of three or four birds. Then he'd head back into the battle, ten to thirty miles away.

Most days the birds came home to the lofts and I was waiting. There was a little can wrapped around each pigeon's leg and I'd unfasten it as soon as the bird had its corn and water. Then I raced with the message to the signal trooper. Most of the messages told the men on the big guns where our foot-soldiers were. They told the gunners where to drop their shells to clear the enemy out of the way and not kill our own men.

The men in my troop said we'd be in Germany by November. 'There's nothing going to stop us now,' the messengers told us when they came to collect the birds.

But Pa always had this saying: 'If anything *can* go wrong then it *will* go wrong.' And Pa was right.

It started when a soldier from the 77th Battalion limped into our camp. He was a big man for a runner – most of them were little fellers. But this one looked like a boxer, battered face, fists like tins of plum-and-apple jam, and broken teeth.

'Birds,' he said to me.

'How many, sir?' I asked.

'I'm not a sir. I'm Private Owens of the 77th. Friends call me Wolfie because I eat like a wolf.'

'I'm Private Clay,' I said. 'Friends call me Dummy because I'm stupid.'

'I'm not your friend. Get me three messenger birds.'

'Yes, sir – I mean, Wolfie.'

He grabbed me by the front of my uniform and lifted me off my feet. His nose was an inch from mine. 'You're not my friend. It's Private Owens to you.'

I glanced at his shoulder. 'You're bleeding, Private Owens,' I said.

'A machine-gun bullet caught me on my way here. The enemy are closing in to cut off the 77th. That's why I need to hurry.'

'But the doctor can look at that, can't he, while I find three birds?'

He grunted, and lowered me to the ground. Wolfie was a rough, hard man but I liked him, so I found my three best birds. Of course you just want to know about the best and bravest of them all, the black one the Brits called Cher Ami. They told me that was French for 'Dear Friend'.

I didn't want to send Cher Ami into the fighting. Some birds didn't come back alive. But I put him carefully into the basket with the other two.

I lived to be glad I did that.

Chapter 5
Bandages and bullets

Wolfie Owens came back from the hospital tent with his arm in a sling, raging and ranting at the sergeant.

'How can I fight with my arm bandaged up like that?' Wolfie asked.

'You were told to stay in the hospital for a couple of days to let the wound heal,' my sergeant said.

'My company is under attack and low on food,' the big man said. 'You want me to lie on a bed in a hospital while my friends starve and get shot at?'

'Yes. You can't help them if you can't fire a rifle.'

The big fists were tight. 'But they need to get messages out. I have to take the pigeons back to them,' he argued.

'You can't carry a rifle and a box of pigeons.'

'I can try.'

I stood watching the argument with the basket in my hands and the three birds making a soft 'coo-coo' sound.

The sergeant caught sight of me. 'Trooper Clay here can carry the pigeons to the 77th. He's a runner.'

Wolfie took a deep breath to hold in his temper and looked at me. 'Trooper Clay?'

'Yes, sir?'

'Have you ever been close to the battle front?'

'No, sir.'

'Do you know the way?'

'No, sir.'

Wolfie turned back to the sergeant. 'See, sarge? Hopeless.'

The sergeant gave a grim smile. 'In that case you can both go. The Dummy can carry his birds and you can show him the way.'

Wolfie looked at me and spread his huge hands. I shrugged. 'I suppose so,' he said.

'I suppose so,' I said.

I packed some food, put the pigeon basket on my back and climbed into a lorry. We clattered over broken roads for twenty painful miles then the driver stopped. 'This is as far as it goes.'

Wolfie stepped down and looked into the distant, dark-green hills. 'See that forest over there?'

'Around five miles off?' I said.

'We walk.'

The autumn fields were soft with rain and shattered by shells. Slimy green water gathered in the shell holes and the smell was sour as one of Pa's pig pens.

We reached the top of a hill and looked down into a valley. Wolfie pointed. 'The 77th were down there when I left them. There are Germans to the right and Germans to the left as well as straight ahead.'

I nodded, and felt a sharp blow to the top of my head as a bullet struck my helmet. If I hadn't dipped my head just then, it would have emptied my brains onto the muddy grass.

I stood there like the dummy they called me. Wolfie grabbed my arm and threw me to the ground. I felt the pigeons flap and squawk as their basket tumbled. But the strangest sound was Wolfie Owens laughing.

'I was shot,' I groaned. 'What's so funny?'

He wiped a tear of laughter away. 'I said there were Germans either side and straight ahead. Well, I was wrong. There are Germans behind us as well. We're cut off, Trooper Clay. Welcome to the 77th, because they're our only hope. If you know how to run then get down this hill and into the trees as fast as you can.'

I picked myself up, strapped on the pigeons and ran for my life.

Chapter 6

Puddles and prayers

Gunfire crackled like a dry log on our kitchen stove back in Kansas as I ran towards the shelter of the trees.

Behind me, Wolfie was walking backwards, firing his rifle from the hip, to make the enemy keep their heads down till I reached safety. He was risking his life to save the pigeons.

The enemy were keeping their heads so low they couldn't see where they were firing but the machine guns were rattling like woodpeckers.

I got a shock when a pale face appeared from behind a bullet-beaten tree. 'This way, soldier,' an American trooper cried. He had a tattered uniform and a scarred helmet.

I sprinted towards him, jumping over tree roots and skidding in muddy puddles, till at last I had the massive tree between me and the machine guns.

Wolfie wandered in after me. 'Hi, Crow,' Wolfie said to the soldier. 'This is Dummy.'

'Pleased to meet you, Dummy... and really pleased to meet your feathered passengers. This way.' The man led us through bushes into the strange stillness of the wood.

Wolfie crunched through fallen branches. 'They call him Crow because he's ragged as any scarecrow you ever met.'

'We're in a bad way, Wolfie. The Germans are all around us. We have no food, not a lot of bullets, and no way of getting help... till now.'

'We'll get a message out this afternoon,' Wolfie promised.

'If help doesn't arrive in two days we're finished. Every day the Germans creep closer and more of the men get shot. The only water is in a stream in a little valley. The Germans have a sniper watching it every minute. We send a man down to get water and we never see him again.'

We followed a path like a thread through the trees. At last we came to a clearing with a few dozen torn tents and some soldiers sitting around looking as miserable as turkeys on Christmas Eve.

An officer strutted across the clearing. He was a small man with thin hair and round spectacles with wire frames. 'Who have we here?' he said, looking at me.

'Private Joe Clay, sir. Messenger.'

He patted me on the shoulder. 'Good man. I'm Major Whittlesey. Let's not waste any time. Get a bird ready and I'll write out a message.'

I fed the birds a little corn as he wrote down six numbers. 'That's our map position,' Wolfie explained.

Then the major wrote, 'Cut off. Low on food and bullets. Send help as soon as possible.'

I took the small slip of paper and folded it so it fitted the small can on the bird's leg. The weary troop of men gathered to watch as I lifted the pigeon over my head and threw it upwards. Two hundred grey faces looked up. Some of the pale lips moved as if they were saying prayers.

The bird soared above the trees and began to fly in wide circles. It was looking for its way back to the pigeon loft. There were rifle cracks from the hillside above us.

The pigeon fell from the sky. Two hundred men groaned.

Chapter 7

Splinters and stones

That night was the worst I'd ever known. Men moaned in their sleep from pain or hunger. From time to time shots rang out as the enemy crept through the moonlit trees and our guards fired.

I slipped down to the stream at the bottom of the bank. I filled cans with water and waited for a bullet to hit me. That bullet never arrived. But the waiting was terrible.

The major decided to send the second pigeon at first light, before the enemy were awake. But as the sky turned a pale pigeon grey, a heavy shell landed at the edge of the camp, tore away tents and wounded more of the troop.

I found Wolfie helping to bandage Crow's leg where a splinter of shell had hit

him. 'The Germans are using the heavy guns on us now.'

Crow said, 'That wasn't a German shell. It came from the west. It was an American shell.'

'They're firing at us?' I gasped.

'They're firing at us because they don't know we're here. Get that pigeon away and tell them to stop,' the man moaned. His uniform was in shreds too tattered for any scarecrow.

The major was scribbling a note that I fastened to the second pigeon's leg. He was a silvery colour and seemed too bright in the rising sun. A man with a rifle should not be able to hit a flying pigeon. But the Germans had a wonderful shot. I hoped he was still asleep.

He wasn't.

The pigeon rose. There was a single shot.

The bird hung in the air and then dropped like a stone.

There was a shriek and a rush of air that tore through the branches above us as another shell came from our American gunners. We were sheltered by the trees but pieces of shell rained down on us and sliced and stung. Crow gave a weak chuckle. 'You all look as ragged as me now.'

I pulled the last pigeon from its basket.

45

I could feel his heart beating in fear, and struggled to hold him as the message was wrapped round his leg.

'Pray this one's luckier,' the Major said, grim and red-eyed behind those thick glasses.

'He's called Cher Ami,' I said.

'Let's hope Dear Friend makes it back to our dear friends.'

I threw Cher Ami into the air. The bird flapped and twisted, and perched on the stump of a tree, lost and afraid. Wolfie jumped to his feet and picked up some of the branches that the last shell had blown down. He began to throw them up at Cher Ami.

He gathered stones that clattered into the tree below Cher Ami's perch. The pigeon turned his little ink-pool eyes on him and stretched his wings, ready to fly if one came too close.

Other men picked themselves up and joined in the effort. At last Cher Ami fluttered and took off. He began his circles to find the way home. The men cheered.

There was a single shot.

The black pigeon spread his wings and glided back down towards the trees, not hurt, but not going anywhere.

'Our last hope,' the Major muttered.

'Fly, Cher Ami, fly!' I cried.

Some men said it was a miracle. I like to think that pigeon heard the voice of the boy who'd fed and cared for him for weeks.

Either way, those wings started to beat and lift him into the morning sky of lemon and scarlet. He wheeled around, searching. Then he flew straight. To the west. To his loft.

Maybe the German rifleman had as big a surprise as we had, because Cher Ami was on the way home before he could shoot again. The men in the camp hugged one another and gathered round to slap my back. 'Fly, Cher Ami, fly,' they cried and laughed.

'What now?' Crow asked.

'We wait,' the Major said quietly. 'We wait.'

Chapter 8

Darkness and deer

It was a week before I found out what happened.

It took Cher Ami an hour to fly those twenty-five miles back to his loft. When he landed a buzzer sounded. An officer looked in the loft in to see which of the birds had come home.

Cher Ami was lying on his back and covered with blood. He'd been blinded in one eye and shot in the breast. His leg had been shot and was hanging on by a thread. And on that thread was the major's message – the message that saved two hundred lives.

Cher Ami had somehow lived to fly home. It was the miracle that our men had been praying for.

We knew Cher Ami had reached the loft with our message when the heavy shells stopped falling.

But it would take time for a rescue group to get through. That afternoon it started to rain. With the tents torn we slept in the mud and ripped up our vests to make bandages.

Night came and I saw shadows of our enemy behind every tree. In the cloudy moon every twig looked like a rifle pointing straight at me.

I don't know if I slept. I talked to Wolfie and Crow about what we'd do when the war ended.

'I think I'll raise pigeons,' I said in the damp dark.

'I'll help you,' Crow offered. 'I'll grow corn to feed them.'

Wolfie laughed. 'You can stand in the middle of the corn field and be your own scarecrow.'

Crow was annoyed. 'What are you going to do on our pigeon farm?'

'Eat them,' the big man chuckled.

The longest night of my life passed with laughter.

When the sun rose the Major gave me a rifle and sent me to the edge of the clearing on guard. He was weary and red-eyed. 'If you see the enemy, pull the trigger. You may not hit him but at least we'll know where the attack is coming from.'

The morning dragged by. Everything that moved scared me. I almost fired at a squirrel, a blackbird and a frightened deer. When I saw the face of a man I closed my eyes and squeezed the trigger.

'Cut that out!' came a cry from the green gloom of the trees. 'We're here to help.' The voice was American.

I think I cried.

The rescuers had cleared a path through the enemy that let us walk the twenty-five miles back to our camp. We ate good hot

food but at first it made the men's empty stomachs sick. We limped on broken boots till they found us some new ones. We carried the wounded over the rough fields.

It took us three days to make that trip. Some of the men were so weak we had to stop and rest every mile. At last lorries arrived to carry us.

When we reached the camp I saw the most amazing sight. Every soldier and officer stood in a line that stretched a hundred yards to the camp gates. The lorries stopped and we walked that last stretch. And every step we took was cheered and clapped by the waiting troops.

'What's going on?' I asked Wolfie.

'They're calling us the "Lost Battalion",' he said.

'It looks like we're heroes,' Crow said.

But for me there was just one hero.

Chapter 9
Pigeon and peg

'We saved his life,' the doctor said. 'I patched up his chest. He had a hole big enough to put your thumb in. I don't know how he flew twenty-five miles like that.'

'Courage,' I said.

The doctor led the way into the medical hut where Cher Ami lay on a bed of straw. His eye looked dull, but I'll swear that when he heard my voice it went bright and he struggled to stand up.

'What's that?' I gasped.

The doctor smiled. 'His leg was wrecked, so one of the guys made him a wooden leg.'

'He saved us all,' Wolfie said.

'You wouldn't eat this little star, would you, Wolfie?' Crow asked.

'Eat him? I'd pin a medal on him.'

The doctor nodded. 'You're not the first to say that. The French Army want to give him their Cross of War – a hero's medal. The press all want his picture. As soon as he's fit enough to travel he'll be taken back to America.'

And that's how Cher Ami became a hero. Me? They checked up on me and found I was too young to fight. Wolfie and Crow were sent back to the front lines. I hope they got through the war all right.

They sent me home on a troop ship. Cher Ami went on a fine ocean liner with a US Army General to wave him off.

I only got to see that feathered fighter once more. Ma drove us down to Great Bend about a year after the war was over. We picked up a newspaper and there was a picture of Cher Ami on the front page.

He'd died in September 1919. Pigeons don't live all that long anyway, but his wounds finally did for him.

Now, you and I die and get buried. But not a hero pigeon. Cher Ami's little one-legged body was stuffed and they put him in a glass case in the National Museum of

American History. I went to see him there. Just the once. To say goodbye.

Life is tough. Sometimes Kansas dust storms wreck our crops. Sometimes I just want to give up. That's when I look up at my pigeons in the sky and half close my eyes, and I think I see Cher Ami up there.

'Hello, buddy,' I say. 'You kept going with one eye, one leg and a hole in your chest.

I can keep going through a little old dust storm.'

That's why we need heroes. They remind us that things are never that bad.

We need that. And it doesn't matter if that hero is a man, a woman, or the bravest bird that ever flew.

Cher Ami.

Did you know?

Messenger pigeons were very important in World War I. Nineteen out of twenty got through. Over 100,000 were used in the war.

Some of these pigeons became quite famous among the soldiers. One pigeon, named The Mocker, flew 52 times before he was wounded. Another was named President Wilson. He was hit by a bullet in the last week of the war and it seemed he could never reach his loft. Though he lost his foot, he made it and saved a large group of American soldiers.

A pigeon named Cher Ami spent several months in the battles of Autumn 1918. He flew 12 times to carry messages.

The most famous was on October 3, 1918. Major Charles Whittlesey's troop of Americans was trapped behind enemy lines. Not only were their German enemies firing at them but their American friends were firing shells at them too. Somehow they had to get a message to their comrades. The only way was by pigeon. But every time a pigeon rose in the air it was shot down. The Americans had one last pigeon, Cher Ami. He was shot down but somehow managed to rise again. He flew 25 miles in just 65 minutes, helping to save the lives of the 194 survivors. He'd been shot through the breast, blinded in one eye, covered in blood and with a leg hanging only by a tendon. Army doctors saved his life. They could not save his leg, so they carved a small wooden one for him. When he was well enough, he was put on a boat to the United States, a hero.

His one-legged body is still on display at the National Museum of American History in Washington, D.C.

What next?

1.   World War I is famous for the poems written by some of the soldiers. Some are terribly sad. John McCrae from Canada wrote about the white crosses on the graves and the red poppies that grew among them:

'In Flanders fields the poppies blow
Between the crosses, row on row'

Edward Thomas wrote about,

'Rain, midnight
rain, nothing but the wild rain.'

Find poems by soldiers like Wilfred Owen, Siegfried Sassoon, Robert Graves or war nurse Mary Borden.

2. Some poems were funny and meant to cheer up the fighting men. They wrote about the awful food, the lice in their clothes. They also wrote about the animals in their trenches. A hero dog called Jim caught trench rats and had his own funny poem.

'A tough little, rough little beggar, and
merry the eyes on him;
But no German or Turk can do dirtier work,
with an enemy rat than Jim'

Can you copy the poem and draw a cartoon to go with it?

3. Can you write your own poem for Cher Ami, the hero pigeon?